SCARY STORIES TO MAKE YOU SCARED OF STORIES

Boo Books, Ltd. Publishers
Los Angeles, CA

Copyright © 2024 by The Boo Boys.

The Boo Boys are Zach Broussard and Nate Fernald.

All rights reserved. No part of this book may be reproduced or transmitted in any form or by any means, electronic, mechanical or supernatural including photocopy, recording, scanning, spells or any information storage retrieval system, without explicit permission in writing from the Author or Publishers.

SCARY STORIES TO MAKE YOU SCARED OF STORIES

PRESENTED BY

THE BOO BOYS

TABLE OF CONTENTS

Warning 1

The Haunted Mansion 15

Nightmare Guy 21

The Clown in the Sewer 25

Mouth Spiders 27

The Exorcism 29

Gen Z Hansel and Gretel 35

Creepy Sounds in the Dark 37

What if Turtles Were Scary? 39

A Story to Scare Your Friends Around a Campfire 41

TABLE OF CONTENTS

The Witch in the Woods 45

The Epic Fail Vid 47

The Buzz 49

Intermission 53

The Diarrhea Song 57

Oh, Fuck. There's a Motherfucking Mummy on the Loose and He Wants to Kill My Ass 61

Creepy Crawly Things 63

The Voice (Not the Show With the Singers, but Think More Like a Scary Voice) 65

The Ventriloquist's Dummy 69

Pet Semetery 71

The Harbinger 77

The Sordid Tale of Vampire Who Lived Next Door 81

A Very Good Kisser 83

The Tale of the Horny Campers Who Were Too Horny for Camp 85

Monster Under the Bed 89

WARNING

This book is scary. It's so scary the authors were forced to self-publish. They sent it to every book publisher and didn't hear back from a single one, presumably because the publishers were scared... to death. Why? Because this book contains graphic depictions of mummies, wolfmans and nasty little men.

It is inadvisable to read this book if you are pregnant, under the age of 57, over the age of 58 or someone who the authors might be romantically interested in.

It is recommended that you use the bathroom before reading this book, as it is clinically proven to scare the shit out of you. At least that's what the authors think their dad meant when he said he "used the pages to wipe his ass."

By proceeding beyond this page, you agree to waive any rights to pursue legal action against The Boo Boys, because they cannot afford it.

YOU'VE BEEN WARNED. Turn the page at your own risk...

Excuse me, did you not see the warning on the previous page? This book is actually fricking scary and it's gonna mess you up hard. You will never be the same person again.

There's still time to read a different book. But if you must, don't say we didn't warn you...

Okay, big man. Seems like you've got something to prove.

Seriously, what are you doing? This book is too scary! We're giving you this warning for a reason, *not* because we're trying to hit a minimum page count!

No one's ever gone this far before. You might be the bravest soul who has ever lived. Continue if you dare...

Okay, looks like we got a real nerd who loves to read! Maybe try going outside and talking to someone for once. There's actually more to life than books – you should try living instead of reading about it, ya weenie.

Congratulations – the previous pages were all part of an elaborate test. And you passed.

We had to bully you to ensure you have the guts to handle the contents of this book. The stories in the following pages are spooky beyond measure. They are not for the faint of heart. And now we know you're ready for the insanity that is *Scary Stories to Make You Scared of Stories*.

THE HAUNTED MANSION

Tim Baxter stared out his windshield, trying to make out the address through the rain. He spotted it, thanks to a flash of lightning that momentarily lit up the night. He checked it again against the business card he'd be given:

GRIEVES & SHACKLETON
667 Devil's Lane
(please note our new address, as we have recently moved across the street)

SOMETHING JUST WASN'T SITTING RIGHT. But then he thought about what the man who contacted him said. If it was true, then this could finally put an end to Tim's financial woes.

He was about to knock, but just before his fist landed on the splintered wood the door slowly creaked open and a strange, excited voice greeted him from the other side.

"Come in! Come in!"

Tim went in and was greeted by a small, wrinkly old man.

"My name is Wendiglion. I was an associate of your great uncle William."

"William... wow, that's a name I haven't heard in a long time," remarked Tim.

"Really? That's surprising. It's a pretty common name."

"I meant this specific William. My great uncle. William Baxter."

"Oh, I thought you just meant the name William in general."

"No."

"Okay."

They sat in silence for forty-five minutes. Wendiglion finally spoke up.

"As you've heard, your great uncle William Baxter recently passed away. William was a man of great wealth but also lived a very secluded life. He had no friends or immediate family. In fact, you are his last living blood relative, which means his entire fortune goes to you."

Tim's eyes lit up. "Really? Wow! This is incredible. Ever since the cup store closed down I haven't been able to get back on my feet. This will solve all of my problems!"

"Not so fast!" Wendiglion said, "There's a catch. Your great uncle William said that before anyone can receive his fortune, they must first spend a night... in his haunted mansion! For decades, no one has been able to spend more than a few hours there before running out screaming. And anyone who managed to stay the night has never been seen again!"

"That sounds really scary," said Tim, "I don't want to do that."

"Then I guess you'll never get your great uncle's fortune!" Wendiglion snipped.

"So then what happens to it?"

"Um... I guess it just stays in the bank?"

"But aren't I his last living relative?"

"Yes..."

"So can't I just get it out of the bank?"

"Well, I mean, I guess. But there's like a whole process you'll have to go through and it's kind of a pain."

"But it can't be worse than staying in a dangerous, haunted mansion, right?"

"It might be? You should probably just stay in the haunted mansion."

"Nah. Too scary. So what do I have to do to get the money out of the bank?"

"You must spend one night—"

"No, not that. The other way."

"C'mon! Your great uncle's dying wish was that someone spend the night in his haunted mansion. Don't you want to honor that?"

"Honestly? I barely knew that guy," Tim mouth-spoke, "I think I met him once at a family reunion or something when I was a kid. People didn't hang around him too much. I mean, he lived in a haunted mansion. He was a real weirdo. Who knows what kind of messed up stuff he did in there? I guess I don't really care about his dying wishes. I just need the money. How do I get the money?"

"Well, first you'll have to acquire a death certificate. Not just for him, but for every one of his relatives. And that's gonna cost you. The price of each death certificate will vary depending on the state in which they died. Theoretically that's all you'd need to do, but the bank won't just let a fortune like this go easily. There's going to be a lot of paperwork involved. In fact, you'll be spending most of your time just proving that there's nobody else associated with his will."

"Yikes," Tim yikes'd, "This sounds like a real headache. I honestly don't know if I'm up for all of this..."

"So you'll be staying at the haunted mansion then?"

"No way. Too scary. I guess I'll just leave the money in the bank to rot."

"It won't rot. They'll assign the account to an administrator."

"An admini-what-or?"

"Stra."

"What's that?" Tim what's-that'd.

"When a person dies and nobody claims their estate, the court appoints an administrator to track down the person who should get the estate."

"Hold on, so you're telling me that if I just don't do anything at all, somebody will basically just come find me and give me all the money?"

"Yes. Or you could spend a night in—"

"No! I'm just gonna sit around until somebody finds me."

"But that could take up to thirty business days!"

"That's fine! It would probably take me that amount of time just to figure out all the paperwork anyway."

"Just stay in the fucking haunted mansion! One night! Quit being such a fucking pussy about it!" Wendiglion shouted.

"Whoa. Dude," Tim whoa-dude'd. Wendiglion composed himself. He was in total disbelief about how much of a dickhead he momentarily became.

"I'm sorry. I... I didn't mean that. It's just... I went to fucking law school. I've passed the bar in seven states. I was top of my class and all I have to show for it is being the guy that tries to get people to stay in some rich weirdo's haunted mansion. Thirty years ago a rich weirdo asks me to deal with his haunted mansion bullshit. I say yes because I need the money, he tells his other rich weirdo friends and then all of a sudden I'm the fucking go-to haunted mansion guy for all these creeps. I'm pathetic..."

"Hey, it's a job," Tim hey-it's-a-job'd.

"I'm better than this. And just talking to you now made me realize how pointless this all is. I don't even have to do anything and people will just get the money. At best, if I do my job right, I possibly send someone to their doom in a haunted mansion. What is wrong with me? I'm such a loser..."

"C'mon, don't be so hard on yourself! You know, now that I think of it, the haunted mansion might be kind of cool," Tim c'mon-don't-be-so-hard-on-yourself-you-know-   now-that-I-think-of-it-the-haunted-mansion-might-be-kind-of-cool'd.

"You're just saying that..." Wendiglion said.

"No, really! How many opportunities am I gonna get to stay in a haunted mansion? Seize the day, ya know? Carpe diem, life is short, Do the Dew."

"You... you really mean it?"

"Yeah. Yeah I do. Now show me to that mansion, Wendiglion!"

"You bet, buddy!"

TIM MADE it four hours in the haunted mansion before being agonizingly ripped apart by ghosts. Like, real bad. They tore his face off. It was terrible. He died.

NIGHTMARE GUY

When the parents of Pine Street found out that local weirdo Edward Burger was hurting their children, they took the law into their own hands. Some suggested burning him alive, while others thought that was too cruel and suggested simply shooting him. They compromised and decided to burn him alive and then shoot the corpse. And that was the end of it. Or so they thought...

That night, Edward showed up in the children's dreams. Any harm he did to them in the dream world would show on their bodies when they woke up. The parents felt helpless to protect their kids in dream world. They knew the kids couldn't fare on their own against Edward. So they burned the local police force alive (and then shot the corpses) so that the police could protect the kids from Edward in dream world. The police took care of him no problem.

But now something even worse was happening. Due to all the sleep they lost from this whole situation, the kids' grades started to slip. So the parents burned a bunch of teachers alive (and then shot the corpses) so that the kids could get extra studying done while they were asleep and get up to speed.

It worked really well. These kids were getting super smart. But to get into a good college you need more than just good grades. So the parents started burning all sorts of people alive (and then shooting the corpses) so their kids could get some real hands-on extracurricular experience. They burned some basketball coaches alive (and then shot their corpses), they burned a community service organizer alive (and then shot their corpse), they burned all the local business owners alive (and then shot their corpses) so the kids could get part time work and internships. They just kept burning people alive (and shooting their corpses) so the kids could learn about anything they wanted.

The kids were absolutely crushing it. Their grades were through the roof, they were in peak athletic shape and they had more life skills than most adults. The parents wanted to reward their kids for all their hard work, so they burned Machine Gun Kelly alive (and then shot his corpse [with a machine gun, just for a fun bit]) so that he could do a concert for them in dream world. He played all their favorite songs and even hung out with them a bit afterward. The kids were so psyched about how down to earth he was.

As the days went by, the parents found that their kids preferred dream world to the real world. I mean, who wouldn't? They had all their favorite stuff, but because it was dream world they could also do things like fly or grow a giant pair of tits. The parents missed their kids and wanted to spend more time with them. It only made sense for them to move to dream world as well. So they burned themselves alive. But they weren't able to shoot their corpses (because they were already dead from being burned alive). And I guess it's the shooting the corpse part that sends people to dream world. Who knew? So they just straight-up died in the worst way possible for no reason at all.

With no adults left or any sort of infrastructure, the whole town really went to hell. A lot of bad, scary people started moving in and it became a real nasty place. Now the kids were less safe than ever. Yikes!

THE CLOWN IN THE SEWER

School ended early because of the heavy rains. As Little Billy walked home, he heard a voice call to him.

"Hey, kid..."

He looked around but didn't see anyone so he continued on his way.

"Hey, kid... down here!"

Aiming his eyes downward, he saw the face of a clown in the storm drain.

"Come here, kid. I need to talk to you."

Little Billy was scared. He'd seen this in a movie and knew how this would end, so he raced home as the clown kept calling out to him.

"Come back, kid! Please! Come back!"

———

MARVIN THE CLOWN died several hours later from a combination of hypothermia and drowning. He was just a regular clown who dropped his phone in the sewer and got stuck when he tried to get it out. And now he's dead. He was also on his way to work at the children's hospital, where he was a doctor.

Sometimes scary stuff can actually just be regular stuff and then you run away and something messed up happens. Now every time you see something scary you're gonna be like "Wait... is that actually a scary thing or is it a regular thing that I'm running away from and turning into a messed up thing?" That's gonna happen for the rest of your life now. Sucks, doesn't it?

MOUTH SPIDERS

They say an average of eight spiders crawl into your mouth every night while you're sleeping. But what they don't tell you is how many spiders crawl into your butthole.

It's 4000.

THE EXORCISM

The room was shaking and the air was filled with the wails of the poor girl's mother.
"The power of Christ compels you!" shouted Father Prine.

With a face covered in boils, the young girl writhed as the demonic force was pulled from her body. This was the most difficult exorcism Father Prine had ever dealt with. He doused the girl in holy water and once again shouted "The power of Christ compels you!" and through the young girl, the demon shouted at him "I fucked your mother in Hell!"

That's when Father Prine knew he was winning. Demons would use this tactic to distract him whenever they were on the verge of being exorcised. This gave Father Prine the burst of energy he needed to continue on.

"The power of Christ compels you! The power of Christ compels you!"

A scream came out of the girl—now in her own voice—as the demon was leaving her body. He heard the demon shout one last desperate phrase at him before the job was done.

"I fucked your mother in the bathroom at the Ashland Chili's just off route nine!"

And with that, the demon was gone. The winds of Hell subsided and the girl began to lightly sob. She had been through so much.

"Thank you, Father!" said the girl's mother, "You have saved our daughter. Can we offer you money?"

"Money won't be necessary, miss. I'm just glad that malevolent presence has finally left our plane."

"He was pure evil. The words he shouted through our daughter were just vile."

"That's very common of Satan's minions."

"And that thing he said about your mother and Chili's? That was just weirdly specific."

"Yeah... I guess it was. That's demons for ya, though. Always trying to rile you up."

Father Prine departed but couldn't stop thinking about what that young girl's mother said. That thing about the Chili's was weirdly specific.

"WOULD you like some more tea, dear?"

"No thank you, mother."

On the first of every month Father Prine visited his elderly mother. They would always have a wonderful time catching up and talking about life. But today Father Prine was awfully quiet.

"Is something wrong, son?" his mother asked.

"No, I'm okay. I think I'm just hungry."

"Why don't we go out and get some lunch? It's been so long since I've actually gone out for a meal."

"That sounds great," Father Prine didn't want to say what he said next, but he couldn't help himself, "How about Chili's?"

At the mere mention of the word "Chili's" his mother's eyes lit up.

"Chili's! Oh, I used to love Chili's. I went there all the time when I was younger and it's been so long since I've been back."

"Really? What kind of stuff did you do at Chili's?"

"Oh, you know. Chili's stuff. Ordered apps. Ate the apps. That kinda stuff."

"Interesting..." Father Prine responded, particularly unnerved.

"Okay, enough is enough. Something is clearly wrong — you never act like this. Please talk to me!"

"It's nothing. It's just that you seemed really excited when I mentioned Chili's."

"Who wouldn't be? It's Chili's!"

"And you're sure you never did anything else at Chili's besides order apps and eat the apps?"

"What else would one do at a Chili's?"

"I don't know. Did you do anything in the bathroom at the Chili's in Ashland off route nine?"

The room went cold. Father Prine's mother was stunned silent.

"What are you getting at?" she asked her son.

"Oh no, it's true, isn't it?!"

"What's true?"

"You fucked a demon in the bathroom at the Ashland Chili's off route nine!"

"I was young! We all do crazy things when we're young!"

"But not have sex with demon's in the bathroom at the Ashland Chili's off route nine! How could you do this when your son is a priest?!"

"You weren't even born yet! You wouldn't be born for almost another year!"

A chill ran down Father Prine's backbone.

"Almost a year? Exactly how long before I was born was this?"

His mother suddenly got very uncomfortable.

"Oh, I don't know..." she stammered.

Father Prine's world crumbled around him. It was all too obvious now. He had never known who his father was and his mother would never talk about it.

"You had sex with a demon in the Chili's bathroom and you didn't even use protection?!"

"I couldn't! Their dicks are weird shapes and condoms don't fit!"

"I can't talk to you right now."

Father Prine stormed out of the house and drove off into the night.

LATER THAT NIGHT Father Prine found himself at the Ashland Chili's off route nine, tossing back one Tito's Watermelon Spritz-Rita after another in between bites of his Tripple Dipper combo platter. It was the first time he'd had alcohol in years and it was hitting him fast. He started ordering everything off the apps menu — Southwestern Eggrolls, Boneless Buffalo Wings, Fried Mozzarella Sharables and even a plate of Texas Cheese Fries.

Suddenly, he felt a presence next to him. He turned to see the blurry outline of a woman.

"That's a lot of apps for just one guy," she said, "Mind if I have a few bites."

Father Prine nodded. The woman began to eat the apps at a voracious speed. Then she looked him right in the eye and said "I have to use the bathroom" and winked at him as she walked away.

"Like mother, like son..." Father Prine said to himself as he walked towards the bathroom.

When he opened the door, the woman screamed.

"What the fuck are you doing?!"

"Oh! I'm sorry! You said you had to use the bathroom and..."

"Yeah, I just ate twelve fuckin' mozzarella sticks and I'm shitting my brains out. What the fuck did you think I was doing in here?!"

Father Prine left the Chili's that night and they never saw him again.*

He was banned because he didn't pay his tab and walked in on a woman shitting.

GEN Z HANSEL AND GRETEL

Hansel and Gretel thought they were going to die in the woods, until they came across an interesting house made entirely of Flaming Hot Cheetos.

"Yeet," shouted Hansel.

"This house is a whole ass mood," shouted Gretel.

Just when the siblings began to go goblin mode on the house, a witch appeared flexing in some vintage drip.

"Bussin' house, right squad?" the witch said like a total girl boss. "I'm vibing inside if you want to kick back. No cap."

But the witch was cap. The witch was very, very cap.

While the outside of this Flaming Hot Cheeto house hit different, the inside was sus, fam. The children immediately saw a big yikes cauldron in the middle of the room, and a book of spells that gave them the ick. The curtains were cringe. The dusty shelves were giving yuck.

Things escalated from sus to wack when the chuegy-ass Karen was all like, "I'm in my villain era."

First she locked Hansel up in a cage that was mid. Then she made Gretel her simp!

The lame-ass asked Gretel to put Hansel in an oven, but Gretel was all like, "OK, boomer." And then Gretel shoved the witch right into, you guessed it, a Skibidi Toilet.

IF THIS DIDN'T MAKE sense to you, you're probably old. You are low-key finna die soon. Slay.

CREEPY SOUNDS IN THE DARK

Snap...

A branch snapped outside. The man was reading in his room silently, but now his ears waited for any other noise.

Creak...

The door to his house was opening. The man could have sworn he locked it.

Thump. Thump. Thump.

Footsteps. Something was walking up the stairs!

Clanklanklankalankank, poof poof poof clank.

It sounded like someone was jump-starting an old Ford Fiesta?

Fluuuuuuuuuuurp.

Pudding getting slapped on a belly?

Skidoink, wamp, wamp, weeeeeeee....

A pogo stick jumping on a butt?

Zwizz, zwizz, pop, pop, splammah-lammah-ding-dong!

Okay, no fucking clue what that was. But the noise was coming from the room next to him. He had to check it out.

Creak...

The man opened the door to his bedroom and saw something truly shocking. His wife was doing some major porking with Michael Winslow, the guy from the *Police Academy* movies who could do all of those crazy sound effects with his voice.
Thud.
The man got so upset he died.

WHAT IF TURTLES WERE SCARY?

Think about it. Make these fuckers a little faster and give 'em some big ass claws. You see one of them out in the wild and you're fucked. They got those shells on their backs so you can't do shit about it. You even think about landing a kick on one of these dudes and your foot is absolutely *fucked*. Now give 'em some sort of nasty scream and nasty little red eyes and it's over. Can you even imagine that shit?

You've got to admit, that would absolutely suck.

A STORY TO SCARE YOUR FRIENDS AROUND A CAMPFIRE

(This story is meant to be read aloud to your friends around a campfire so that you can scare them. The parts in parenthesis are instructions on how to best scare them. Do not read these parts out loud! If you've already started reading this part out loud, then you're pretty much fucked. You ruined it. Your friends are going to have a bad time and it's your fault.)

Todd had been working in the old folks home for about a year. There was a woman named Ethyl in his wing. She always sat by herself staring out the window and nobody ever visited her. But the thing that made Todd take notice of her was the giant diamond at the end of her necklace. It had to be worth a fortune. When Ethyl finally died, Todd took the necklace. It was the perfect crime. Or so he thought...

A week after she was buried, Todd was working late one night and saw that Ethyl was sitting back by the window again. She kept repeating the same phrase over and over.

"Where's my necklace... where's my necklace..."

Todd was terrified. But when he took one more step closer, she said...

(*Okay, now's the time to scare your friends. When you read the next line, shout it as loud as you can while grabbing your friend's wrist.*)

"You have it! Give it back!"

(*That must have really scared your friends, huh? But that's nothing – you're about to really freak them out. Look one of your friends directly in the eye and now place your hand into the fire. Leave it there for at least twenty seconds and don't say anything. Now ignore your pain and just continue reading the story like nothing happened.*)

Todd ran as fast as he could. He rushed to his car, but when he got to the door he noticed that Ethyl was now sitting in the driver's seat.

(*At this point, your friends should be freaking out pretty hard. They'll probably be trying to get you to go to the hospital, but that's only because the story has really scared them. They're just using it as an excuse to get you to stop reading the story. Do not listen to them! Instead, take a burning log out of the fire and eat the whole thing. It's gonna be pretty hard, but just don't be a fucking baby about it. Once you've downed the entire log, continue reading the story.*)

She kept repeating the same phrase over and over.

"Where's my necklace..."

"I'm sorry!" Todd shouted, "I don't know where it is!"

(*When you read this next line, shout it as loud as you can and stick your hand into your friend's pocket.*)

"You have it!!"

(*Do not remove your hand from your friend's pocket. Instead, start licking their face. And continue reading out loud.*)

I just went whole hog on the log and your head's next, pretty boy.

(*Now your friends will probably all be trying to physically subdue you. This means you have really scared them. They may* have even called an ambulance because your hand and mouth are looking pretty bad. You'll most likely have some internal bleeding as well from eating a whole ass log. They will probably take this book away from you, so hold on tight and try really hard to memorize the rest. Continue to read/recite as they all pin you down.)

Todd tried to run away, but Ethyl's grip was too tight.

She continued holding on to Todd while demanding her diamond back, causing Todd to die of fright.

After Todd died, Ethyl found a piece of paper in his pocket. It was a receipt that said who he sold the diamond to. It was someone named...

(Now say the name of one of your friends, then point behind them and say "There she is!" Your friends will all be so scared as an ambulance and police car arrive to take you away. As the officers pin you down and the paramedics attempt to treat your wounds, shout the following line.)

I know where your mothers sleep! I know where your fathers piss! I'm out for blood!

(Keep shouting this as you are dragged away. Once the sirens fade, your friends will all remain pretty shaken and slowly start to discuss the events of what happened. They will try to figure out if there were any signs leading up to your apparent breakdown, but there weren't. Then after they head inside and get ready for bed they'll notice something in their pocket... a large diamond!)

(Ah, shit. I forgot to tell you in the beginning that earlier in the day you should have put a large diamond into each of their pockets. Dammit. I fucked up – my bad. Sorry you're in the hospital.)

THE WITCH IN THE WOODS

Tyler had dreams of becoming a famous movie director. After graduating from film school he just couldn't get his foot in the door in Hollywood. He knew he needed to make something good to get the attention of movie executives. But as an upper middle class suburban kid, he didn't feel like he had any interesting stories to tell.

On a visit home, Tyler was reminded of the Briar Woods — a dense patch of trees behind the slaughterhouse that nobody dared go in since several kids had gone missing there years earlier. There were rumors of an awful creature living in there known as the Briar Witch. Tyler finally had his idea — he was going to go into the woods with his camera and catch the Briar Witch on film. This would be his big break.

He took out a hefty loan so he could hire a crew and rent equipment. Then he set off into the woods.

His dreams were about to become a nightmare.

Tyler never found the Briar Witch and now spends his days editing prank videos for a YouTuber in order to pay off his loans. It's the worst job he's ever had. Sometimes the scariest thing of all is real life.

THE EPIC FAIL VID

I always loved watching fail videos on the internet, until I saw the man fall on "Epic Ass Bust – Watch Til End".

The moment the man on the video busted his ass, I jumped in my seat. The jet-black hair. The goatee. I recognized the man from another fail video. He was the guy who jumped off that roof toward a pool but missed the water. He busted his ass there, too.

In a matter of days I saw more videos with the man. He was in "Loser Smashed In Nuts By Drone" and one time he swung a golf club so hard he lost his balance and fell into a lake.

My heart skipped a beat when I saw the video where he forgot to put his car in park and chased it down a street. I saw familiar signs along the road. This guy was from my town.

I became fixated on finding the man, and finding out if he was okay.

It took a few weeks of scrolling through online maps, but I finally found a house I recognized from most of the videos. When I got to the house, there was a shiny black Cadillac in the front yard. Was the man faking fail vids for money? Does that mean he's okay?

I was caught off guard by the sweet older woman who answered the door. I explained the man I was looking for, medium build with black hair and a goatee. She smiled.

"My son is very popular on the internet," the old woman said. "Would you like to meet him?"

The old woman led me behind the house and I found myself nervous to meet a celebrity of sorts, and thrilled to confirm he was doing just fine. Then I realized we were walking toward a shed. My stomach turned when I saw the shed's door was padlocked shut. The old woman smiled and opened it up.

"Michael, you have another visitor."

I stepped forward. It was pitch black inside. There was a cord attached to an overhead light. I pulled it, illuminating the room. Then I screamed.

Inside there were dead bodies of several men, each crawling with maggots and worms, and each with the same jet black hair and goatee. And next to me on a shelf was a bottle of black hair coloring.

"You better get some rest, sonny," she said, "Tomorrow your ass gets epically busted."

THE BUZZ

J ohnny and Kayla were on another road trip when their trusted Nissan Versa sputtered to a stop on a lonely stretch of highway.

"I swear the exit sign said there was a station this way," Johnny said, defending his drive down this desolate road.

They had run out of gas before. But this time felt different. They didn't know this part of the country. It was dark out. There was no phone service.

"What the hell do we do now," Kayla asked, finding it hard not to blame Johnny for this mess.

"Wait for another car to come and ask for help." He tried to sound confident, but his voice failed him.

Johnny knew he should save the car battery, but he popped on the radio anyway. He began scanning for channels.

A local AM broadcast was all they picked up. It was blasting some clangy old country tune about a girl who ran off with another man.

But the song abruptly cut out, and a broadcaster's voice boomed loudly.

"We come to you with reports of a daring escape from

Nightingale Mental Institution. The escaped patient, known as Bobby "The Buzzer" McGillicutty, was being held for life after the deviant Sex Shop Break-In of '02."

Johnny turned the radio off and his skin prickled with gooseflesh.

Kayla sensed his panic and decided to act.

"One of us should walk back to the interstate," she said.

(If you, the reader, assumed the man would be the one to walk off into the darkness, you're wrong. Says way more about you and your expectations of gender roles than it does about the story.)

Johnny watched her walk off into the darkness. He couldn't resist the urge. He turned the radio back on.

"The Buzzer is on the loose," the broadcaster exclaimed. "This man is a pervert, twisted and depraved, and locked away from society for the depraved acts he committed at that sex shop, forcing innocent patrons into unspeakable acts we can't describe over the airwaves."

Johnny shut off the radio and shuddered. Sitting in silence was better than hearing about that terrible pervert.

But it wasn't exactly silent. There was a faint but steady noise coming from somewhere outside.

Buzzzzzzzzzzzzzzzz

Johnny looked around. He couldn't find the source of the buzzing. It was coming from somewhere in the dark. And it was getting louder.

BUZZZZZZZZZZZZZZZZZZZ

Johnny tried his phone. Suddenly there was the slightest bit of reception. One solo bar. He called 9-1-1. The phone rang. There was an answer!

"9-1-1, what's your—"

The reception was cut out. And when the call dropped and the speaker was silent, the noise was suddenly deafening.

BUZZZZZZZZZZZZZZZZZZZZZZZZ

Horror crossed Johnny's face when he realized it. The buzz was coming from inside the car.

———

HOURS LATER KAYLA made it back to the Nissan Versa. She had managed to get a lift at the interstate (from a *female* truck driver!) and returned with a full gas canister.

The windows were completely fogged up when she approached. She slowly opened the door and saw Johnny. But he was hunched over on the dash with a buzzing piece of plastic shoved up his you-know-where (his butt, in case you don't know where).

"The madman," Kayla shrieked. "Did he get my Johnny!?"

Kayla slowly reached out for his shoulder, terrified by how still he was.

Suddenly Johnny's head popped up. He turned his head slowly to hers. He was smiling from ear to ear.

"Ummmmm, yeah," Johnny said. "I guess you could say he got me real good."

The couple drove off into the distance. Some say you can still hear a slight buzzing whenever Johnny's around, from the vibrator that's shoved up his ass.

INTERMISSION
A NOTE FROM THE AUTHORS

Your heart is likely racing from the previous stories and spooks. You are brave for making it this far. As a reward, the authors have left the following page blank to give you a little breather from the terrifying scares.

BOO!

Gotcha, bitch.

THE DIARRHEA SONG

When you're sliding into first
And your pants begin to burst
Diarrhea, Diarrhea
When you're rounding third
And you feel a juicy turd
Diarrhea, Diarrhea

Ever wonder what happened at second base? There's a story there. A scary story. But nearly everyone who lived in the town is dead now, so maybe it's finally safe to share the legend?

The rhyme is based on a real event that happened to a real boy. What happened on second base was so disgusting it was never shared beyond the confines of the small town. All who were there swore to only make fun of what happened to the boy on first base, third base, and home plate. But no one ever joked about what happened on second base. It was too scary.

THE BOO BOYS

IT WAS a beautiful day for a ballgame. The boy's father was home from war. The boy just wanted to make his daddy proud. And when the bat hit the ball, the boy knew right away he had knocked it out of the park.

Many people forget the central contradiction of this story. If the boy "was rounding third with a juicy turd" that means the boy had hit a home run.

His father was beaming from the stands, chanting the boy's name over and over again.

It was great having his dad back. The night before the family ate out at his father's favorite restaurant. It was a hole in the wall called Sloppy John's Milkshake and Day-Old Chili Dogs. They served giant milkshakes and extra long chili dogs that were cooked yesterday and left out.

His first mistake was sliding into first. No one really does that, especially not after hitting a home run!

It was mid-slide that the boy's pants began to burst. The stands fell into a deep silence as they watched the boy (who just hit a home run) lay silently, tummy down, with his hand reaching out to the bag.

The boy mustered up the strength to stand up and make his way to second base. The crowd started to clap. They thought he was injured! He looked even better in his father's eyes. He hit a home run and he was also brave.

It was right at second base when the diarrhea came back with a vengeance.

You see, the boy had developed a serious case of lactose intolerance since his dad went away for war. But he was afraid to tell that to his dad. He didn't want to look weak. Instead he chugged the milkshake and ate the day-old chili dogs with extra cheese in silence. Now he was paying the piper.

Diarrhea began to fill the boy's baseball pants. These

were the type of baseball pants that cinch up below the knee, and the diarrhea filled up each leg like two long water balloons.

He stood frozen at second base. To move even an inch would disturb the icky equilibrium and spell certain doom.

It was the sound of the ice cream truck that broke the dam. His stomach turned again, the seams gave way, and it was just like that elevator scene from *The Shining*.

He wanted to make his daddy proud, though. He hit a dinger and he had to finish rounding the bases. That's when he slipped in his own diarrhea and fell flat on his back into all that butt-sauce.

To make matters worse he started to cry for his dad. The boy whimpered, "Daddy, me made a stink stink..."

Also, you should know this boy was seventeen. Can you imagine how pathetic this kid must have sounded?

There was a murmur coming from the stands now. The boy slipped in his squirt a few more times before he finally stood and saw for himself.

The true second rhyme goes as follows:

> *When you cry for pops at second*
> *But daddy left, you reckoned*
> *Diarrhea, Diarrhea*

In a way it's impressive that the boy rounded third at all. The game was already called off and the stands were mostly empty. When he rounded third, he barely felt anything, let alone a juicy turd.

The boy's pants were filled with foam when he finally came into home. It was the last true home the boy ever knew. He ran away and was never seen again.

The events of that day turned into a fun little rhyme, and that rhyme spread from town to town. A dark trend emerged.

When someone was bold enough to share the second base rhyme, they met a shocking and horrific death.

Don't believe me? Go to the bathroom. Look into the mirror and repeat the full diarrhea song, along with the cursed second base rhyme. Smell a little diarrhea? Could be a dirty toilet. Could be leaky pipes. Or it could be the boy with pants filled with foam, coming into your home... to kill.

OH, FUCK. THERE'S A MOTHERFUCKING MUMMY ON THE LOOSE AND HE WANTS TO KILL MY ASS

Well this fucking sucks. I let a fucking mummy out of his pyramid and now he's after my ass. I just wanted to get some treasures and rubies and shit, but now I got this fucker trying to tear me apart. I'm honestly pissed.

What the fuck am I supposed to do? I can't kill his ass, because this fucker's already dead. So I've just been running and running and running and it absolutely sucks shit. I mean, I gotta go to work tomorrow. How the fuck am I supposed to do that? I tried calling my boss and telling him there's a mummy bird-dogging my ass and the motherfucker was like "Just don't be late." You motherfucker. You better hope I don't show up with this mummy on my ass. He'll just start chomping the shit out of motherfuckers all over that place. Get fucking real, dude.

Can't believe how much my life fucking sucks right now. It can't get any worse.

Oh fuck.

No way.

Are you fucking kidding me?

Now there's a fucking wolfman. Shit.

I've got a motherfucking mummy and a motherfucking wolfman both trying to tear my ass apart. This sucks major hole and I'm absolutely pissed about the whole situation.

Here's what sucks the most:

The mummy? That fucker was slow as shit. As long as I walked just a little bit fast he wasn't gonna do shit to me. But the wolfman? This fucker can run. I'm straight up hauling ass now. And I'm gonna have to keep hauling ass until this full moon goes away. As long as I can make it till then, I'll be fine. Gotta stay fucking positive. I can do this.

Oh fuck.

Shit.

No way.

No fucking way.

Are you fucking kidding me?

Now there's a motherfucking Dracula. Fuck.

Mummy, wolfman and Dracula all on my ass. This sucks major chode.

Well, it was nice knowing you all. I had so much fucking cool shit planned for the rest of my life, but I guess all those plans are fucked now.

And here they are. Wolfman fucking biting me, Dracula fucking biting me, mummy doing what ever the fuck mummies do to me. This hurts and it sucks. I'm pissed. Sucks that I have to die being pissed.

Fuck this shit. Fuck mummies, fuck wolfmans, fuck Draculas. They all fucking suck and now I'm fucking dead.

See ya.

Fuck.

CREEPY CRAWLY THINGS

Within minutes of moving into the old house, Toby saw a giant fucking spider.
SWAT.
Killed the son of a bitch, Toby thought.

But Toby shrieked when he saw the baby spiders spread out from the mother spider's corpse. Thousands, no millions, of itsy, bitsy, spiders. They weren't just going up a water spout. They were crawling over all of Toby's shit.

Toby found spiders everywhere after that. In the microwave? Spiders. In the junk drawer? Spiders. On the toilet seat? Piss. (And spiders.) They were everywhere.

At the time things were going well with a girl named Amanda. She had finally come over to Toby's new place. That night she followed him upstairs and Toby thought he was gonna score. But when she unzipped his pants she screamed and ran out of his house. There's no way she screamed because she saw his totally normal dong. He had washed it a week ago and it was totally normal. She must have seen a spider.

Toby lathered himself in cologne and headed to the local

bar to meet someone new. Not a single woman wanted to talk to the "spider guy."

The bartender cut him off after he called a woman the b-word.

"Let me guess," Toby asked. "You won't serve *my kind*?"

The black bartender looked like he wanted to hit Toby hard. But something stopped him. Was it something with eight legs that he was scared to touch?

The next morning Toby was called into his boss's office. There was a big ass security guy there to escort him out of the building because, according to his boss, they found a bunch of weird searches on Toby's work computer. But Toby knew this didn't have anything to do with his searches for "Shrek but with a big hog." This was about the freaking spiders.

Toby had enough. These spiders were ruining his life. He called an exterminator to get the problem taken care of once and for all. They covered his house in a tent and pumped it full of poison for days while Toby slept in a bucket. When the job was finally done he called Amanda and told him the spiders were gone. Would she want to come over now?

To Toby's horror, Amanda replied "What spiders?"

It turns out the spiders weren't the problem after all. Toby was just weird and gross. And on top of that, now he was a spider killer.

THE VOICE (NOT THE SHOW WITH THE SINGERS, BUT THINK MORE LIKE A SCARY VOICE)

It was the first night Julia had the place to herself. All of her roommates were out of town, so she thought she'd make some popcorn and put on a scary movie. Normally she would be watching her favorite show *The Voice* (okay, this is *The Voice* as in the show with the singers, but that's not what this story is about – there's gonna be a scary voice in a little bit), but tonight's episode was a rerun.

Just as she sat down to watch the scary movie, her phone rang.

"Hello?" Julia answered.

"Hello, Julia... do you like scary movies?" asked the voice (this is the scary voice, not the show *The Voice*. Remember – she's not watching that tonight as it's a rerun).

"I do!" said Julia.

"What's your favorite scary movie?"

"Who is this? Is this Trey?"

"No, it's not Trey."

"Alright, is it Damien?"

"Not Damien either."

"What about Alonzo?"

"Nope. Not Alonzo."

"It's gotta be Chaz."

"It's not Chaz."

"Then it must be Doozer."

"Definitely not Doozer."

"Hold on, let me look at my contacts to see who else I know."

Julia then scrolled through her contacts and said all 257 names in there. It wasn't any of them! Not Brian, Kyle, Dodo or even Jammer. It also wasn't Vern or Horp.

"Okay," Julia finally gave up, "Who is it then?"

"I'm not telling..." the voice (scary, not show) said coyly.

"Well I wish you'd told me that at the beginning. Before I said all those names."

"Me too. But I just wanted to say... that's an awfully nice shirt you're wearing."

Julia's heart sank. How could he know she was wearing a shirt? She immediately started locking all the doors in the house.

"Whoever you are, this isn't funny!" she shouted.

"No need to get upset. All I did was compliment your shirt. It's a nice shade of blue."

Julia paused.

"Wait, my shirt's orange."

"Oh... really? Maybe it's one of those things where the stripes make it look like a different color to different people?"

"There's no stripes. It's just plain orange and says 'I'd rather be filling my toilet with old ham.'"

"Filling your toilet with old ham? What does that even mean?"

"Nothing, it's just a funny shirt. Like 'Life is a beach' or whatever."

"Life is a beach makes sense. It's a pun. What is putting ham in the toilet?"

"I told you, it's just a funny shirt."

"Okay, well the shirt I'm looking at doesn't even have words on it. You're at 222 Cheston Street, right?"

"No, I'm at 222 Cheston Lane. Common mistake."

"Oh, okay. Give me a minute."

The voice (scary) hung up.

"Glad that's over with!" Julia said to absolutely no one. She felt relieved until the phone suddenly rang again. Her heart started racing as she answered.

"Hello, Julia... quick question. Is Cheston Road before or after the 7-11?"

"That depends on where you're coming from."

"From Cheston Street."

"Oh yeah! Obviously. It's after the 7-11."

"Just in case, what color is the house? I don't wanna have to call again."

"It's brown with red trim. It's gonna be hard to see in the dark so I'll put the porch light on."

"Awesome. Thanks so much."

The phone call ended.

"Well that was scary! Glad it's over now," Julia shouted directly into the fridge.

She finally began to relax when the phone rang again. Maybe it wouldn't be the voice (scary, not show) this time. Maybe it would be Duke or Fonzo or Gordon. Maybe even Chip or Buzzard. But no, it was the voice again (to clarify, still the scary one on the phone. I know the phrase "the voice again" could be confusing given that there is a rerun of *The Voice*, so technically "*The Voice* again" is happening. But it's not that – it's the scary guy).

"Hello?" Julia asked, quivering.

"Hey, me again. Sorry, but your dog seems a little intense. Will I be okay getting out of my car?"

"You should be, but I'll call him off just in case," Julia stuck her head out the window and shouted "Tae Bo! To your bed!"

"Great, thank you." He hung up the phone.

"Well I'm certainly glad that's finally over with!" Julia shouted into a cup. She briefly felt at ease until she heard the doorbell ring. It was him. How did he find her? She opened the door. Standing outside was a man in a black cloak and a mask that looked kinda like the one from *Scream* but was actually its own, different thing. He pulled out a knife and Julia immediately ran upstairs and locked herself in the bathroom.

But it was no use. He was too strong. The door was kicked in with ease. He held the knife up over his head, but before he struck he noticed that the toilet was full of old ham.

"Wait, what the fuck? Why is your toilet full of ham?"

His momentary distraction was just enough for Julia to kick him in the shin. He dropped the knife, screaming in pain. Julia quickly grabbed it, mustered all of her strength and stabbed herself in the chest."

"No one kills Julia but Julia!" she shouted before collapsing on the ground in a pool of blood next to a toilet filled with old ham.

THE VENTRILOQUIST'S DUMMY

The ventriloquist had been performing the same routine for years. Lately, however, the ventriloquist's dummy was acting strange. Very, very strange. Every time the ventriloquist would slip his arm into the backside of the dummy, the dummy would moan "daddy like."

PET SEMETERY

He wasn't sure if he could trust the old man, but he didn't have a choice. As the wisps of cloud scattered over the midnight moon, Kyle followed the lumbering elder deep into the woods. It was hard to see, but he did his best to follow the sound of leaves crunching beneath heavy footsteps. Then suddenly, there was silence.

"We're here," the old man said.

Kyle looked around. They arrived at a clearing with makeshift gravestones strewn about. Some made from rocks, others from scraps of wood.

"So this is really it... the Pet Cemetery."

"Actually, it's called the Pet Semetery," the old man responded.

"That's what I said," Kyle said.

"No, you said 'Cemetery,' but it's actually a 'Semetery.'"

"You're saying the same word."

"No I'm not, you little asshole. You said it with a C. I'm saying it with an S."

"How can you even tell that?" Kyle asked.

The old man didn't respond. He just stood there until Kyle broke the silence.

"Well, thanks for showing me where this is."

"Don't thank me yet," the old man warned, "They say anything dead buried in the Pet Semetery... tends to make its way back to the living."

"That's the plan," Kyle said, staring at the cold ground.

The old man grabbed him by the collar, staring Kyle dead in the eye.

"Heed my words... when these pets come back, they're not the same as they once were! This place is dangerous. The only reason I even agreed to show you how to get here is because you gave me four dollars!"

"I offered you a hundred!"

"I only needed four!" the old man snapped back. "Well, don't say I didn't warn you."

"I understand. I just really need my pet back. I love my pet. He was such a good pet."

The old man began to walk away. After a few paces he stopped and turned quizzically to Kyle.

"Aren't you coming?"

"Nah, I'm good. But thanks for showing me where this place is."

"Don't you need to get your pet?"

"Right..." Kyle was at a sudden loss for words. "I... I have him actually. Have a goodnight!"

The old man slumped his shoulders and let out a long sigh.

"Oh no... you're one of those guys, aren't you?"

"One of what guys?!" Kyle asked defensively.

"One of those guys who can't get hard anymore and thinks if he shoves his dick in the dirt at the Pet Semetery it'll start working again."

"*Whaaaaaat*? No! That is *not* me! That's not me at all! I'm just a total animal lover lookin' to get his pet back."

"If you insist," the old man responded.

"Now if you'll excuse me," Kyle said proudly, "I need to dig a hole. For my pet."

He pulled a teaspoon from his pocket, put the end of it into the ground and just sort of started turning it. The old man looked suspiciously at him.

"Just curious, what kind of 'pet' are you burying there?"

"It's a... cat," Kyle said.

"Awfully small hole for a cat."

"That is *not* a small hole!" Kyle snapped, "That is a regular sized hole! I don't know what kind of sick stuff you're watching on the internet, but this hole is a completely normal size!"

"And you're gonna fit an entire cat inside that hole?"

"Oh. Right. Did I say cat? I meant mouse. It's my pet mouse, but his name is Cat. Cat Stevens."

"Like the musician?"

"No. My name is Kyle Stevens and he is my pet mouse, Cat Stevens. And I need to get him back. I just really miss the little guy—regular-size guy! Not little."

"So where is he then? Your pet mouse."

"He's... in my pocket."

"Can I see him?"

"No. Because... he was actually hit by a car and it's just a really gruesome scene. We're talkin' full-on mince meat. And I'm afraid that if I show him to you, you'll puke and I just don't wanna see that happen because you look like a guy who eats weird stuff."

"I do eat weird stuff. You ever heard of nut bucklins?"

"No."

"They smell weird but taste good sometimes. I slurp down a few cans of 'em a day."

"You slurp them?"

"Oh yeah, they're *real* wet. Chunky little wet bits," he said while smacking his lips.

"Look, will you *please* leave so I can grieve in peace?" Kyle asked as he began to unbuckle his pants.

"Wait, why are you unbuckling your pants?! If you're trying to tell me that you're not here to pork the ground with your limp dick, then why the hell are you unbuckling your pants?"

Kyle was at a loss for words as he suddenly realized that taking your pants off is not something one would generally do at an animal burial.

"Because..." he searched for the words, stammering out whatever came into his head, "because in the viking religion, the master of the household is known to remove their pants during the grieving process. This act is known to symbolize the freedom that comes with death, while achieving a vulnerability that one can only find when they embrace the fragility of life."

The old man was stunned. This was the most beautiful thing he had ever heard.

"That's the most beautiful thing I've ever heard. I'm sorry I doubted you. I'll leave you be."

The old man started making his way back to the path.

Kyle stood over the hole, staring into it, getting lost in the darkness. Until he realized something.

"Ah, shit," he said, "I dug the hole too big. Now I'm not gonna feel anything!"

"I knew it!" the old man exclaimed as he came running back to the clearing. "I knew you were gonna fuck the ground!"

"Alright, fine!" Kyle confessed, "You got me! Are you happy?"

"Just be warned—it never works out well for people who bury things in the Pet Semetery!"

"'Never works out well?' Buddy, it's half past midnight on a Tuesday and I'm in the middle of the woods trying to shove my limp chode into some dirt. Things have already not worked out well for me!"

The old man took this in.

"Huh... I guess you're right. I never really thought about it that way. Well, I'll leave you to it. Enjoy the dirt!"

The old man left, Kyle enjoyed the dirt and neither of them were ever seen by anyone again. They didn't die, but the next day everyone in the world went blind at the same time. That's actually a much scarier story. Probably should have told that one.

THE HARBINGER

A jeep full of dumb and horny teens roared down a lonely stretch of desolate highway. They were approaching the only gas station for miles. The driver, a dumb and horny teen by the name of Skeez, pulled the jeep next to the pumps.

Suddenly something – or rather, someone – caught his eye. In front of the station there was a man as old as dust rocking away in a rocking chair.

"Reckon you teens are making your way to the Old Duvall Mansion."

The dumb and horny teens were silenced by the old man's voice.

"I wouldn't go in there if I were you. It would be a shame if something happened to your precious little friends."

The man laughed an evil little laugh. Simultaneously a wolf howled in the distance.

No one ever came this way, unless they were going to the Old Duvall Mansion. And they never, ever came back. As the sole resident of the surrounding area, this old decrepit man had taken it on himself to warn all who dared enter.

"We already know about the murders," Skeez said. "We heard all about it on a murder podcast."

That shocked the old man. His whole gig was warning people about the murders.

The pump clicked when the jeep's tank was full. Skeez was about to step into the driver's seat when the old man's voice roared ominously through the barren landscape.

"I wouldn't listen to that murder podcast if I were you..."

It was clear that the old man's heart wasn't in this one. But he tried to look ominous all the same. Thankfully another wolf howled in the distance. It could have been the same wolf, though.

Skeez looked around at his friends, then slowly approached the old man.

"You don't know what a murder podcast is, do you?"

The old man hemmed and hawed, but finally hung his head low. He did not know what a murder podcast was.

"Podcasts are sorta like radio," Skeez said, trying to explain everything in a way an old guy might understand. "And murder podcasts are basically radio programs about murders that make commutes more fun. There's tons of 'em."

The old man was thinking hard now.

"So," the old man asked, "you don't need to be warned about the Old Duvall Mansion—"

"—because we heard about it on a murder podcast. Right."

Skeez actually felt bad for the guy. It was like his job (being creepy) was being replaced by technology.

"Huh," said the old man quizzically, "maybe I'll start a podcast."

A chill ran through the air. The wolf howled. Same wolf? No way to know.

Skeez looked the harbinger in the eye and delivered a cold message.

"I wouldn't start a podcast if I were you." The (a) wolf howled. The old man looked around, confused.

"Why not?" asked the old man, a touch of fear in his voice. "Seems like a fun thing to do. I could really spread the word to people about the Old Duvall Mansion!"

Skeez took a step closer to the old man, an evil smirk spreading across his face.

"You think you can just get a microphone and start a podcast? Without the backing of a major podcasting network or a host that's already famous, you'll never get a fanbase."

The old man was shaking now. "Maybe... maybe I'll have enough listeners to earn some ad revenue. Not to make a living or anything. Just a supplemental income!"

The smile that crossed Skeez's face was cold and menacing.

"Oh, you won't be making any money. Not unless you do... live shows!"

The old man's heart nearly stopped. Skeez let out a maniacal laugh. The wolf(s) howled louder. (Could just be dogs.)

The old man watched as Skeez got back into the jeep full of horny teens.

"You take care now," Skeez said as he waved a knowing goodbye, "and don't forget to... *lock the gates.*"

Skeez laughed. But the reference was lost on the old man, as he had only just heard of podcasts. To him it was nothing more than a random quote from *Almost Famous* made by somebody who was definitely too young to have seen that movie. There the old man stood, more scared and confused than he'd ever been in his life.

THE SORDID TALE OF VAMPIRES WHO LIVED NEXT DOOR

L ong story short, I'm starting to think the people next door who claim to be vampires are just dorky goths who have weird sex with each other.

A VERY GOOD KISSER

Brian's girlfriend booked a modeling job in the big city. Thankfully for her, Brian had an uncle who lived in the big city.

He messaged his uncle. It turned out, the man was going away for the weekend. The apartment would be empty and all theirs.

Part of Brain was relieved the uncle wouldn't be there. Something was always strange about the man.

They arrived to find the place small but tidy. Brian cooked his girlfriend dinner, then they settled in for bed. She needed her rest.

That night Brian had terrible nightmares. Something about sleeping in his uncle's bed brought out strange dreams of this very unusual man. After hours of tossing and turning he found his girlfriend's body in the sheets. She kissed him for a long time. After a nice kissy-kissy, Brian fell into a deep slumber.

When his morning alarm went off, Brian realized he was alone in the bed.

A light was on in the bathroom and the shower was running.

Brian walked toward the sound of running water. But he found the shower empty.

In the bathroom he found a letter from his girlfriend. It read, "Work called right after you fell asleep. I hope I didn't wake you."

Brian was suddenly covered in gooseflesh. If she left right after he fell asleep—

The bathroom was steamy now, and on the mirror was a message written just for Brian.

UNCLES CAN KISS TOO!

Brian shivered. Come to think of it, he probably should have noticed something was up when he felt all of that stubble during the kissy-kissy sesh. That's on him.

THE TALE OF THE HORNY CAMPERS AT CAMP WHO WERE TOO HORNY FOR CAMP

Over the course of the first eight weeks of summer camp there had been 13 slayings. Two teens making out in the boat shed were bludgeoned with an anchor. Even a counselor, while peeking into the girls' showers to get his rocks off, was strangled with a hose.

The counselors called an emergency meeting. Danny, a first year camper, knew it had something to do with the murders. The rumor spreading among the kids was they had ideas on how to stop them.

Head Counselor Rick addressed the gathering.

"Howdy ho, campers!"

The entire group of kids returned a hearty "howdy ho!"

"As you might have heard," Counselor Rick began, "there's been a series of twisted and sadistic murders that have threatened to shut down our summer fun."

The kids booed. They, just like Danny, wanted the summer fun to never end. Counselor Rick smiled, then calmed the group down.

"Looking back," Rick said, "we noticed the only campers

left unscathed were those who didn't engage in sexual activity. So we're instituting policies to keep our summer safe by ensuring none of the campers, or counselors, under any circumstance, gets horny."

Danny did not want to die. If all it took was not getting horny as a thirteen-year-old boy, he was sure he could do it.

"First and foremost, campers have to start covering up their legs. That's why all campers, especially you ladies, will have to wear knee-high socks."

Danny jerked with a sudden squirm in his seat.

"Ummmmmmmmmmmm..." Danny raised his hand politely. "Some campers, not me but somebody else who's not me, might find the knee-high socks to be sexy. It could actually make them hornier."

The counselor nodded, taking in the information seriously.

"Great point," Counselor Rick conceded. "Let's flip the script. No socks at all. No shoes at all. Just our bare, nasty feet out in the open."

"Ummmmmmmmmmmmm..." Danny's hand was back up. "Interesting idea! No such thing as a bad idea, but I think that some people, who are not me so let's just give that idea up, they might be sexually attracted to feet."

Danny looked around with a giggly panic. "I'm just trying to keep an eye out for the freaks, you know?"

The counselor considered it seriously.

"Good thinking," Rick said. "We're not stopping there, though. Tomorrow you'll notice a few staffing changes. From here on out, all of the younger, hotter counselors will be replaced by older women. And they won't be wearing skimpy outfits. They'll be wearing formal business attire to make sure none of you, under any circumstance, gets horny."

"Ummmmmmmmmmmmmm... about that." All eyes turned to Danny now. "Basically," Danny explained, "I have this friend, who is not me but does have a similar vibe, and this guy had his sexual awakening at a JC Penny lingerie section. Basically, his mom made him wait outside the dressing rooms for her, while these absolute smoke shows tried on blouses and pantsuits, all while I–I mean he–softly touched the lace braziers."

Counselor Rick was frustrated at this point.

"Why don't you just stand up and address the entire group."

"I can't do that."

"Why?

"No reason! Just spitballing ideas here."

Head Counselor Rick grasped for options.

"Okay, what if counselors completely covered themselves up."

"That could work."

"They could wear full-body anthropomorphic animal costumes."

"Ummmmmmmmm..."

"They would look like life-size cartoon animals. It wouldn't be sexual at all."

"I'm gonna frickin' die this summer! I mean, my friend is gonna frickin' die this summer!"

The room erupted into a panic. They were all afraid of being murdered. Being murdered is sort of the worst thing that could happen in life.

Counselor Rick had an idea. It was a crazy one, but it could save their lives.

"Camp was canceled last summer," Rick pointed out. "The chili had gone bad. Everyone got terrible diarrhea when it was served on the first day in the canteen. If we serve last year's chili, everyone will get diarrhea. It'll be a miserable summer, but at least no one will get horny."

Everyone turned to Danny. He tossed the idea around in his

head for a bit. Maybe it was an idea so crazy it just might work. But then, suddenly and with a wild rage, Danny squirmed with a lustful thrust.

"Ummmmmmmmmmmmmmmmmmmmmm..."

MONSTER UNDER THE BED

I am the monster under the bed. I feed off of fear, waiting for the perfect time to strike. For years, I have been laying under this young boy's bed. Every creak and scratch he hears at night is caused by me. Every chill that goes through his body makes me stronger. My strength gathers every sleepless night. I've grown powerful.

Tonight... I strike.

IT'S NOW HIS BEDTIME. I watch his every move from under the bed as he shuffles from dresser to closet, making sure no dangers lurk. For the first time, he locks his door. He must really be scared. His slippered feet move just inches from my claws as he climbs into bed, having no idea what awaits — clueless that this is his final night on earth.

He pulls the covers tight, but they won't save him. Now is my time to—

Wait, what's that sound?

Oh no.

Oh god.

He's jacking off.

Shit. Dammit. I've always eaten the kids before they hit puberty. Not totally sure what to do in this case. I guess I'll just wait until he's done? Yes. He'll be done soon. And then...I shall feast!

Okay, sounds like he's done. Now is the time for the darkness to strike. This shall be his last—

What the fuck? He's jacking off again.

Okay, I can handle this. I've waited years to eat this kid. What's another ten minutes? Soon he'll be done. And then I shall feast and become more powerful than I have ever—

Oh my god, he's doing it *again*?! Three times in a row? This kid is sick! How is this even possible?

I'm just gonna close my eyes and wait for this to be over. Please be over soon. Please...

———

I SHOOT awake at the sound of a creaking floorboard, adrenaline rushing through me. It sounds like he's done. I can hear him downstairs in the kitchen, rummaging through the refrigerator. He must be charging up for another round. I've got to get out of here.

As I climb out from under the bed, I see his laptop. Every instinct tells me not to, but I can't help but glance at the screen. It's worse than I thought.

PREGNANT MILF STUCK IN WASHING MACHINE

Are you kidding me? This is the first time this kid is masturbating and that's what he's watching? This can't be good. Where do you even go from there? Well, I don't plan on sticking around to find out. I have to get out of here now.

I make my way towards the door.
Creak.
Shit. I know that sound all too well — the hallway floorboard. I'm too late. He's on his way back.

I dive under the bed. He'll be asleep soon and then I am out of here.

The sound of him climbing into bed, once the source of my powers, now sends shivers down my spine. What have I become? Go to sleep, child. I'm begging you.

And then I hear that horrible sound.
Click.
No. Not another video. It can't be. He is more monster than I.

There is not an ounce of fear left in him. This will be my life for years to come.

What is this sick feeling inside of me? Is it judgment of this boy?

No. It's something worse.

It's fear.

My kind are not supposed to know fear. As I feel it creeping into me, my life force begins to shrink. I am dying.

As my consciousness fades, I am cursed with one final image in my mind. The last thing I will ever see or know before being snuffed out of existence.

PREGNANT MILF STUCK IN WASHING MACHINE
PREGNANT MILF STUCK IN WASHING MACHINE
PREGNANT MILF STUCK IN WASHING MACHINE
PREGNANT MILF STUCK IN WASHING MACHINE
PREGNANT MILF STUCK IN WASHING MACHINE
PREGNANT MILF STUCK IN WASHING MACHINE

CONGRATULATIONS

By finishing this book, you have proven that you are one of the bravest people on earth. Braver than all frontline workers combined. You're undoubtedly covered in your own piss and shit right now and probably still crying. But the completion of this book means you are now officially a Big Strong Boy™.

But there's something you should know...

THIS BOOK IS CURSED. All who read it are condemned to live a life of utter torment, inviting demons from the furthest reaches of our world to haunt their dreams. There is, however, a way to break this ancient curse. Head over to Amazon.com and leave a five star review for *Scary Stories to Make You Scared of Stories* and the demons should fuck off real quick. One to four stars will result in more demons. Choose wisely...

Sincerely,
The Boo Boys

Made in the USA
Middletown, DE
24 October 2024